This book belongs to

_____

MICKEY'S WORLD OF WORDS

bird   fork   car   farm   friends   broom

Disney's
READ and GROW LIBRARY

Published by Advance Publishers
Winter Park, Florida

Written by Susan Cornell Poskanzer   Edited by Bonnie Brook
Penciled by Jeff Shelly   Painted by Arkadia Illustration & Design Ltd.
Designed by Design Five
Cover art by Peter Emslie
Cover design by Irene Yap

ISBN: 1-885222-81-5
10 9 8 7 6 5 4 3 2 1

One day Mickey and Goofy decided to go on a *bicycle* ride, but they couldn't decide where to go.

helmet

seat

bell

bicycle

basket

2

handlebars

pedal

wheel

Then Goofy looked around Mickey's yard.

"Hey, let's go find things to build a tree house!" he said.

"That's a great idea," said Mickey.

So off they went on their bicycles.

First they pedaled out to a *farm* and found things to use in their tree house.

"We can use this old wood," said Mickey.

barn

silo

corn

rooster

farmer

hay

hen

horse

tractor

cow

4

"We can use this weather vane," said Goofy. "Looks like someone threw it out."

Then they pedaled through a *small town* and found things to use in their tree house.

"We can use these sticks," said Mickey.

"We can use this old piece of rope, too," said Goofy.

mail truck

mail carrier

fence

mailbox

neighbor

chimney

house

lawn

7

telephone

fire hydrant

street

traffic
light

building

train

bus

police
car

taxicab

sidewalk

Next they pedaled through the *city*.

"We should build a door like that one on the grocery store," said Goofy.

"And a window like the one on the bicycle shop," said Mickey.

bird

statue

They pedaled through
the *park*.

Mickey looked at all the
people. Goofy looked at a little
yellow bird, high up in a tree.

tree

fountain

boat

pond

garden

"Goofy, watch out!" yelled Mickey.

"Huh?" said Goofy. But it was too late. Goofy hit a tree branch. He fell off his bicycle and scraped his elbow.

They made a quick stop at the *doctor's office*. The doctor put a bandage on Goofy's elbow. Goofy was very brave.

eye chart

stethoscope

doctor

"I feel better already," said Goofy. "Thanks, Doc!"
"Thank you, Nurse," said Mickey, as he waved good-bye.

nurse

cotton
balls

flashlight   bandages

13

Then they stopped for lunch.

"We'll go to your favorite *restaurant*, Goofy," said Mickey. "You can rest your scraped elbow there."

waiter

pitcher

glass

sandwich

fork

plate

knife

tablecloth

napkin

"Great," said Goofy. "And I'll have my favorite lunch, too—a peanut butter sandwich."

"I'll have soup," said Mickey.

spoon

bowl

menu

They made a quick stop at a *construction site*. They saw all kinds of machines and the workers who use them.

construction worker

bulldozer

sign

HARD HAT AREA

"Look at that big dump truck!" said Goofy. "Look at that bulldozer!"

"Gosh!" said Mickey. "They make me want to go home and start on our own building project."

"You're right, Mickey," said Goofy. "Let's go."

dirt

dump truck

power shovel

hard hat

steam roller

STOP sign

STOP

So they pedaled carefully through *traffic*.

"We need to buy some tools," said Mickey.

curb

crosswalk

18

shoppers

crossing
guard

ONE WAY

WALK

WALK
sign

car

wrench

screwdriver

saw

hammer

pliers

ladder

folding ruler

They went to a *hardware store* and bought tools to build a super-duper tree house.

"Our tree house will be the best!" said Goofy.

20

paintbrush

nails

paint roller

drill

"That's right," said Mickey.
"It WILL be the best!"

"Maybe we should get some groceries for later," Mickey said.

"Good idea! I sure get hungry when I work," said Goofy.

So they made one last stop at the *grocery store*.

PRODUCE

bananas

potatoes

lettuce

grapes

apples

onions

tomatoes

carrots

DAIRY

soup

eggs

milk

bread

fish

cheese

As soon as they got home, they parked their bicycles in the *garage*. Then they unloaded all the building tools, materials, and groceries.

They were almost ready to start building their tree house. They had just a few more things to do.

broom

garden hose

dustpan

leaf blower

garden cart

garbage cans

24

shovel

hoe

lawn mower

25

First they went to the *bathroom* and washed their hands.

soap

washcloth

sink

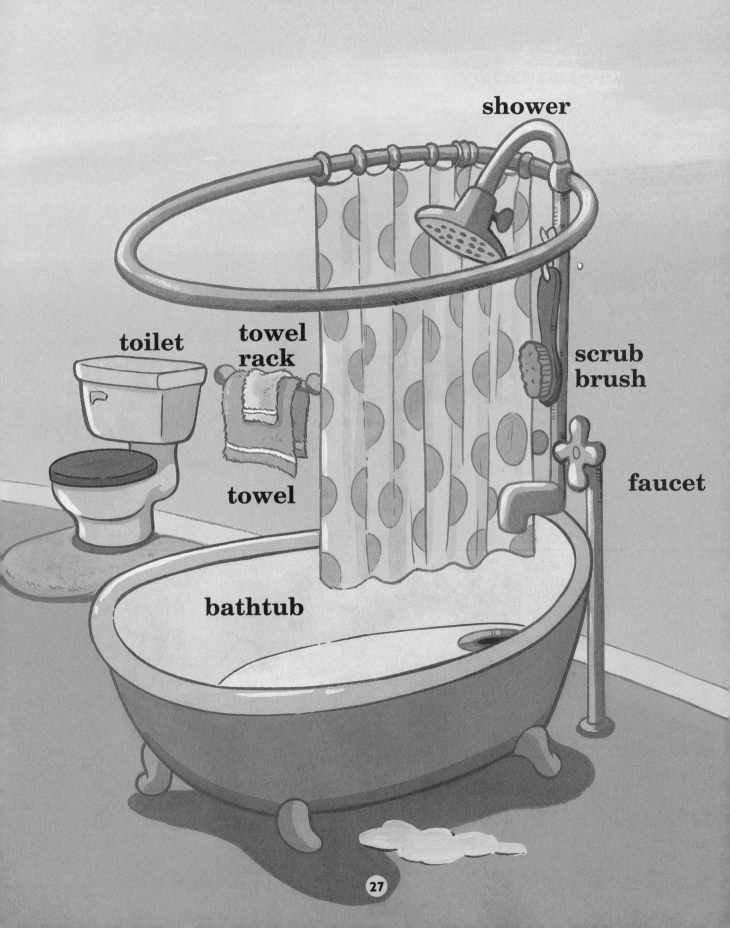

shower

toilet

towel
rack

scrub
brush

faucet

towel

bathtub

Next they went down the hall to Mickey's *office* where they drew up plans for their tree house.

Then they went through the *house*, collecting things they needed to build their tree house.

Goofy went to the bedroom, the bathroom, and the living room.

attic

bedroom

living room

Mickey went to the attic and the kitchen.

"You can't use a lamp in the tree house," said Mickey.

"Oh, yes I can," said Goofy.

bathroom

kitchen

Finally they dressed in their *work clothes*. Then they went out to the backyard to choose the best tree for their tree house.

cap

T-shirt

socks

shoes

"How about that one over there?" asked Mickey, pointing to a tree that was not too short and not too tall.

"That's perfect!" said Goofy, smiling.

work gloves

overalls

sneakers

squirrel

caterpillar

So Mickey and Goofy worked and worked. All the *animals* in the backyard watched them.

bee

butterfly

worm

Mickey and Goofy built and built. They painted their tree house all different *colors*.

red

orange

green

black

Finally they sat in the *backyard* to rest.

"Gosh, our tree house sure is, well . . .
interesting," said Mickey. "Especially your
side, Goofy."

birdhouse

swing set

sandbox

seesaw

"Do you know what I'm going to do?" Goofy said. "I'm going to bake a cake, and invite all our friends over to celebrate!"

"That's a great idea," said Mickey. "But please, let me bake the cake."

doghouse

Goofy agreed to let Mickey bake the cake, but Goofy was the one to invite all their friends over for a big *party*.

friends

party hats

candles

ice cream

cake

balloons

presents

And everyone agreed that the tree house was the best
they had ever seen.

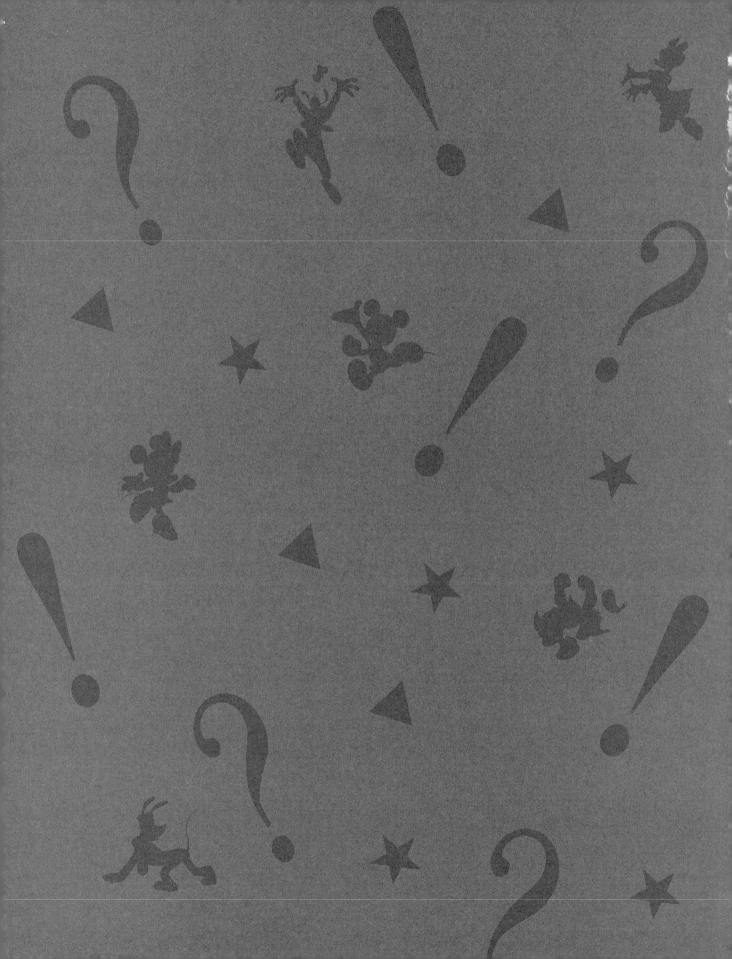